Max and Morgan's ABC's

Written by Debra A. Cavanaugh, R.D.H.
Illustrated by Robin W. Meldrum

Halo ●●●●
Publishing International

Max and Morgan's ABC's
First Edition March 2009
Text Copyright © 2009 *Debra A. Cavanaugh, R.D.H.*
Illustrations Copyright © 2009 by Robin W. Meldrum
ISBN 13: 978-1-935268-00-0
Library of Congress Control Number: 2009924447

Please Visit Debra Cavanaugh at:
www.cavanaughbooks.com
or
www.halopublishing.com

Published by

Halo
Publishing International
www.halopublishing.com
Telephone (216) 255-6756

Printed in the United States of America

A is for April

April is Max's mommy's birthday.
"When is your birthday?"
She wrote this book for you so you can learn
your ABC's with Max and Morgan.

This story is about Max the best dog ever!
One day in March he came to the Cavanaugh house in
Willoughby, Ohio. That is where Debra and Dennis live.
Morgan arrived in June and came for a visit.
Soon…Debra, Max and Morgan became best friends forever!
I wonder what Max's favorite thing is to eat?
I wonder what Morgan's favorite color is?
See if maybe they are your favorites, too.

B is for boy

Max the dog is a boy. His birthday is December 30th.
His favorite blanket color is blue with white and red stripes.

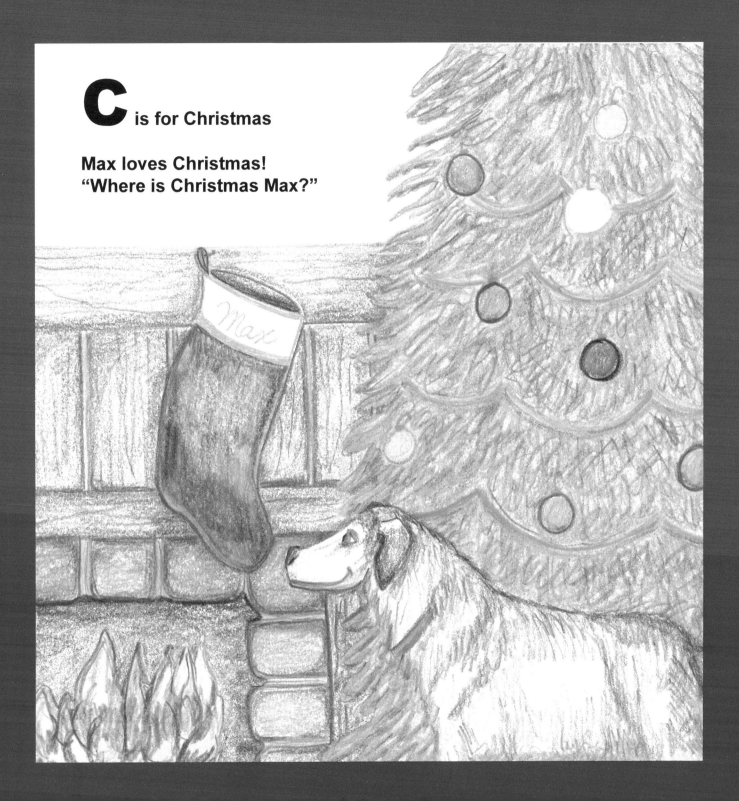

C is for Christmas

Max loves Christmas!
"Where is Christmas Max?"

D is for dog

**Max is a good dog.
His birthday is in December when all
the snow falls.**

E is for eat

Max and Morgan like to eat meatballs.

F is for fish

Max caught a fish!

G is for grass

Max and Morgan love to lay in the green grass and play.

H is for howl

Max loves to howl at the T.V. and when Morgan comes over.

I is for ice cream

Max and Morgan love to eat ice cream cones.

J is for June

**Morgan's birthday is in June.
She loves to jump rope.**

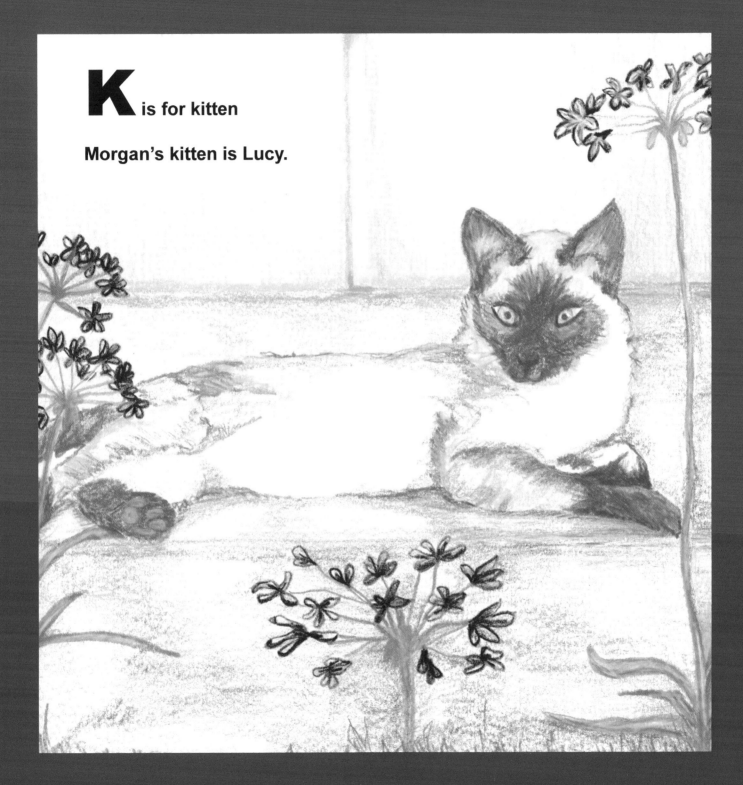

K is for kitten

Morgan's kitten is Lucy.

L is for loves

Everyone loves Max and Morgan!

M is for mud pies

Max helps Morgan make mud pies.

N is for November

November is the month Max and Morgan love to celebrate Thanksgiving and eat turkey.

O is for October

October is the month for "Happy Halloween!"
Morgan says, "Max can not have any candy!"

P is for pool

Max and Morgan love to swim in the big blue pool.

Q is for quiet

Quiet … it is nap time!
Max and Morgan like to sleep on Max's favorite blanket.

R is for ribbons

Morgan likes pink ribbons in her hair.

S is for snow

Max is a snow dog with big beautiful blue eyes.
Max and Morgan love to play in the snow and catch snowflakes.

T is for toys

Max and Morgan have tons of toys.

U is for umbrella

Max and Morgan sit under the umbrella to get out of the sun.

V is for vegetable

Max and Morgan's favorite vegetable is broccoli.

W is for water

Max and Morgan love to play in the water.

X is for x-rays

X-rays are pictures that can be taken of your teeth.
Max's mommy cleans and takes x-rays of children's teeth like you!

Y is for you

I hope you enjoyed this story!

Z is for zoo

Morgan loves to visit the zoo.
Her favorite animal is the zebra.

Printed in the United States
148422LV00005B

This book is dedicated to:

Special pets:
Max and Mia
Bear, Scout and Zoe.

And to all children who are truly loved.
I hope you will laugh and have fun
learning the alphabet for many years to come.